In memory of Nana and Pop
—C.F.

To Ellie and Bethany with love
—R.T.

E
FRE

Production Manager : Diane Sahadeo
Library of Congress Cataloging-in-Publication Data

Freedman, Claire.
Good night, sleep tight / Claire Freedman ; illustrated by Rory Tyger.
p. cm.
Summary : While babysitting, Grandma tries several ways to get Archie to
feel sleepy but nothing works until she remembers how she used to put
his mother to bed when she was a little girl.
ISBN 0-8109-4513-4
[1. Bedtime—Fiction. 2. Grandmothers—Fiction. 3. Bears—Fiction.]
I. Tyger, Rory, ill. II. Title.
PZ7.F87275Go 2003
[E]—dc21
2002155049

Text copyright © 2003 Claire Freedman

Illustrations copyright © 2003 Rory Tyger

Published in Great Britain 2003 by Little Tiger Press
An imprint of Magi Publications
1 The Coda Centre, 189 Munster Road, London
SW6 6AW

Printed and bound in Belgium

10 9 8 7 6 5 4 3 2 1

Harry N. Abrams, Inc.
100 Fifth Avenue
New York, N.Y. 10011
www.abramsbooks.com

Abrams is a subsidiary of
LA MARTINIÈRE
GROUPE

Good Night, Sleep Tight

by

Claire Freedman

illustrated by

Rory Tyger

HARRY N. ABRAMS, INC., PUBLISHERS

One night, Grandma was baby-sitting Archie. "Aren't you sleepy yet, Archie?" asked Grandma.

"No!" replied Archie. "I don't feel sleepy at all. I'm wide awake!"

Grandma sat down on the edge of Archie's bed. "Have you got all your favorite friends to snuggle up with?" she asked. "They might help you feel sleepy."

"I've got Tiger and Rabbit,"
said Archie. "But where's
Elephant?"

"Here he is," said
Grandma, tucking Elephant
in nice and snug. "Hold him
tight and soon you'll feel
sleepy."

But neither Archie
nor his little friends
went to sleep.

"We're still wide
awake, Grandma," he said.

"What about some nice
warm milk?" said Grandma.
"That makes me feel ready
for bed."

Archie drank every drop of his milk, but he didn't feel sleepy. "I'm still wide awake, Grandma!" he said. "Please can we watch the fireflies? That might make me feel ready for bed."

Grandma wrapped up Archie in his cozy
blanket, and together they watched the
dancing fireflies. Archie tried to count
them, but it didn't make him feel tired.
"I'm still wide awake, Grandma!" he
said. "Would you sing me a lullaby,
please? That might make me sleepy."

Grandma sang some of Archie's favorite songs. Archie closed his eyes and listened . . . but he didn't feel sleepy. "I'm still wide awake, Grandma," he whispered.

"I know, Archie," Grandma said. "Let me rock you in my arms. That will make you sleepy."

Grandma rocked Archie gently in her arms, all the way down to the apple grove and back. Archie felt safe and warm in Grandma's arms, but he didn't feel the tiniest bit sleepy.

"Grandma, I'm STILL wide awake!" he said. "Will you tell me a story, please? Listening to stories makes me feel sleepy."

Grandma sat down comfortably,
and Archie snuggled up close
to her.

She told him stories about all the naughty things his mommy had done when she was as little as he was.

"Your mommy never felt sleepy at bedtime either," Grandma said.

Grandma carried Archie back inside. She smiled a secret smile as she remembered putting Archie's mommy to bed when she was little.

Grandma tucked Archie into bed. She pulled the covers right up to his nose.

"I used to tuck your mommy into bed, with the blankets pulled right up to her nose—like this!" said Grandma.

"Then I'd stroke the top of Mommy's forehead— like this," Grandma said.
Very gently she stroked the top of Archie's forehead.

"And I'd give Mommy a very special good-night kiss," said Grandma.

Grandma gave Archie a special goodnight kiss.

"That's right, Grandma," said Archie with a big yawn. "And then she says, 'Good night, sleep tight!'"

"That's right, Archie," said Grandma . . .

And before Grandma could even say "Good night, sleep tight," Archie was fast asleep!